Also by Shirley Hughes
Alfie's Feet • Alfie Gets in First
Alfie Gives a Hand • An Evening at Alfie's
Another Helping of Chips • Chips and Jessie • Dogger
Here Comes Charlie Moon • Moving Molly • Up and Up

The Nursery Collection: All Shapes and Sizes • Bathwater's Hot
Colors • Noisy • Out and About • Two Shoes, New Shoes
When We Went to the Park

For Dorothy Briley

Library of Congress Cataloging in Publication Data
Hughes, Shirley. The big Alfie and Annie Rose storybook.
Summary: Presents experiences of nursery school
student Alfie and his younger sister Annie Rose.
[1. Brothers and sisters—Fiction] I. Title.
PZ7.H87395Bi 1989   [E]   88-11149
ISBN 0-688-07672-6 ISBN 0-688-07673-4 (lib. bdg.)

THE BIG
ALFIE AND
ANNIE ROSE
STORYBOOK

SHIRLEY HUGHES

LOTHROP, LEE & SHEPARD BOOKS
New York

Breakfast

Early one morning Alfie helped his baby sister, Annie Rose, out of her crib, and they went downstairs. Alfie went down forward, holding on to the banister. Annie Rose went down backward, feet first.

Dad was in the kitchen having his breakfast, so Alfie and Annie Rose joined in and had breakfast, too. Alfie sat at the table in a proper chair. He had a china bowl with bears marching all around the edge. Annie Rose sat in her high chair with the tray in front. She had a plastic drinking mug and bowl and her own little spoon.

While Alfie was eating his cereal, Annie Rose
pretended she was playing in a band. She drummed
her spoon on the tray — ring-a-ding, bong-a-bong —
and sang very loudly, "Morra, morra, morra, gorra,
Doo-lay!"

Dad hid behind the cornflakes box when Annie
Rose was singing and playing because it was so noisy.

When Alfie had eaten as much cereal as he wanted, he
made patterns in his bowl. He made the crumbly bits
into an island with a sea of milk all around. But soon the
island got all soppy and soggy, so he gave each bear a
piece of it with the tip of his spoon. After that his
breakfast looked rather messy.

Then Alfie kindly started to help Annie Rose with her breakfast. He filled her drinking mug with milk. Annie Rose could drink out of it very well by herself. But when she'd had enough, she started to drip the rest onto her tray and onto the floor. Dad got a cloth and mopped it up.

Annie Rose could eat out of her bowl when she wanted to. Alfie helped her fill up her spoon.

But today she couldn't make up her mind where her breakfast was supposed to go. She tried putting it into her ear, then into her hair. Then she started to spread it all over the place. Quite a bit of it went down her front.

"Put it here, Annie Rose," said Alfie, opening his mouth very wide and pointing.

Then Annie Rose opened her mouth very wide, too, and put in a big spoonful of breakfast all by herself.

"Look! Annie Rose is eating up her breakfast!" shouted Alfie.

"Eating is quieter than singing, I suppose," said Dad.

Grandma's Pictures

Alfie and Annie Rose had a grandma. She drove
about here and there in her little red car, and she often
came to visit them. Sometimes she brought presents,
even when it wasn't anyone's birthday.

Grandma could dance,

and she could sing

and tell stories.

She and Alfie did a lot of cooking together.

Grandma had a big book of pictures. There were photographs of everyone in the family. Alfie liked looking at them with her and asking who all the different people were.

There was a picture of Grandma and Grandpa on
their wedding day, and a picture of Mom when she
was a little girl and another when she was a big
schoolgirl. And there was a picture of Mom and Dad
at the seaside, before they got married.

There were some pictures of Alfie and Annie Rose,
too, when they were tiny babies. The one Alfie liked
best was a picture of himself having a bath in the old
baby bathtub.

The oldest picture in the book was rather faded. It was of Grandma and her brother Will when *they* were children. That was a very long time ago. Alfie liked hearing Grandma tell about what things were like then, when they lived in the country and didn't have a car or a television set. Grandma and Will had to walk a long way to school every day, along a green lane with hedges full of wild flowers and blackberries on either side.

Grandma liked school even though the teacher was very strict. Grandma's brother Will was older than she was, but he didn't like school one bit. As they got nearer and nearer to school every morning, Will would walk more and more slowly. Often, Grandma said, she had to drag him along by the hand or they would be late. Sometimes they would arrive at school only just in time, as the school bell stopped ringing.

Will hated school so much that one morning, do you know what he did? He took off his gray school trousers and threw them over the hedge!

It was a very high hedge, so there was no hope of getting them back again. Then he walked on, and up to the school door, in his underpants.

Of course, when the teacher saw him like that, and with all the children giggling, she wouldn't let him come into the classroom. He had to stay in the boys' cloakroom all morning, and at lunchtime she sent him home in a pair of borrowed trousers. They were much too big and had to be held up with suspenders.

But Will didn't mind. He got what he wanted, which was the next day off from school. You see, Grandma explained, he had only one pair of good trousers. Their mother wouldn't dream of letting him go to school in anything else, and so she had walked up the lane herself and climbed over a high gate into the field to rescue Will's trousers. They were all dirty and covered with cow-pat.

The next day their mother washed the trousers and hung them on the clothesline to dry while Will stayed indoors and played with his new jigsaw puzzle.

"Does Will still live in the country and have no car and no television?" Alfie wanted to know.

"Oh, no," said Grandma. "He grew up long ago and went off to live far away in Australia. Now he has a big car and a television, and he owns a store where he sells men's and boys' clothing."

"Does he have trousers in his store?" asked Alfie.

"Oh, yes," said Grandma. "Many, many pairs."

Statue

When Alfie and Dad go to the park,
they always see
the big stone man,
sitting high up
in his stone chair.
Down below,
Alfie and Dad
chase each other
round and round,
creeping round corners
and jumping out—
Boo!
The stone man doesn't move.
He doesn't notice
even when a bird sits on his head.
At night,
when everyone has gone home
and the park is closed
and it's dark all around,
he's still sitting there.

Proper Words

Annie Rose could walk quite well, but she couldn't talk properly yet. She could say only four words. They were "Mommy," "Daddy," "no," and "more." The rest of the time she talked in a private Annie Rose language, which nobody else understood. She talked to her toy lamb, and she could turn the pages of Alfie's picture books and read stories aloud, using lots of different voices. And she was very good at getting people to understand when she wanted something.

In the mornings when Mom went to collect Alfie from nursery school, she took Annie Rose along. Annie Rose was very interested to see all the children coming out of school. Her favorite person was Alfie's best friend, Bernard. Whenever she saw Bernard, she shrieked with joy and waved her arms and kicked her legs about. Bernard wasn't very polite to Annie Rose. He would pop out his eyes at her and move his jaw from side to side and gibber like a chimpanzee. Annie Rose didn't mind. She just laughed and laughed at Bernard's funny faces.

One day Bernard and his mom came to visit.
The moms sat in the kitchen and drank tea and
chatted while Alfie and Bernard went off to play
together. Annie Rose wanted to join in, but they
wouldn't let her. They hid behind the curtains and
kept as quiet as mice while Annie Rose went about the
room looking for them. She couldn't find them
because she wasn't very good at looking.

When Annie Rose gave up and settled down to play on the floor, Bernard shouted, "Quick, there's a crocodile!" Then he and Alfie jumped up onto the sofa and pretended that they were on a rock in the middle of a river and Annie Rose was a crocodile in the water, coming to eat them up.

Annie Rose tried to climb onto the sofa, too, but they pulled up their legs and pretended to be frightened. Annie Rose didn't understand their game. She wanted Bernard to make funny faces at her.

"Goo gorra da!" she said.

"Why don't you teach your baby to talk properly?" Bernard asked Alfie.

"I'll teach her if you like! Who's that?" said Bernard to Annie Rose, pointing at Alfie. Annie Rose didn't answer. She just pointed at Alfie, too.

"What's my name, then?" Bernard asked her next. Annie Rose answered in Annie Rose language. It sounded like "Borra Blodder Doon."

"No it's not, it's Bernard," Bernard told her. "Bernard, Bernard, BERNARD!" he shouted, and each time he said it he hid his face in a cushion and popped out at her. Annie Rose thought that was a wonderful joke, and she laughed and laughed.

When it was time for Bernard to put on his coat and go home, Annie Rose was upset. She held him tightly around the waist, wanting him to stay and make more funny faces at her.

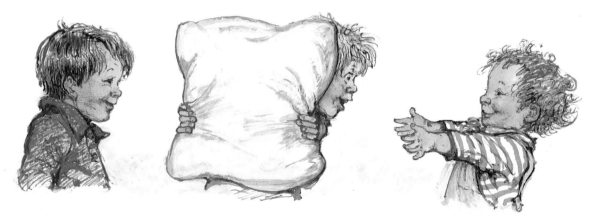

The next day when Annie Rose and Mom
were waiting for Alfie outside nursery school,
Bernard was the first to come out. He was wearing
a paper hat, which he'd made that morning. He
had painted big eyes and rows of pointed teeth on
it. When he saw Annie Rose, he spread out his arms
and swooped down at her, making loud zooming
noises.

Annie Rose smiled. She kicked
her feet and held out her arms.
"Dernard!" she said.
Bernard stopped zooming.
"Dernard!" said Annie Rose
again, very loudly and clearly.

"I do believe Annie Rose has learned to say your
name, Bernard," said Mom, surprised. "I never heard
her say that before." Then all the moms and dads
who were waiting too stopped chatting and smiled at
Annie Rose.

"Dernard!" said Annie Rose firmly, pointing at
Bernard and looking around at everyone. She was very
pleased with herself.

"I've taught your baby to talk," Bernard told Alfie when he came running up to join them. Alfie didn't think much of Annie Rose's cleverness. To tell the truth, he was rather annoyed that she hadn't learned to say *his* name first. She was *his* baby sister, after all.

Annie Rose soon learned to say Alfie's name and many other words, too. But from that time Bernard always made special faces for her when he came out of school. Sometimes he even let her hold on to his hand. When he came to play at Alfie's house, he put her into a cardboard box and shoved her about all over the kitchen floor. Annie Rose liked that better than anything.

"More, Dernard, more!" she would shriek happily.

People in the Street

A lot of people
live on Alfie's street.
There's Mrs. MacNally,
polishing her door knocker,
and Maureen,
mending her bike;
and Mr. MacNally,
lying under his car
with only his legs sticking out.
Here comes Gary,
whizzing up and down,
showing off his new roller skates,
and Debbie Jones and her mom,
going to the shop.
A lot of people go past Alfie's house:
the milkman,
and the window washer,
people going to work
and coming back.
And there's the little dog
who barks a lot,
but he's quite friendly, really
(I think).

Mr. MacNally's Hat

One morning Mom took Alfie across the street to Mrs. MacNally's house to be looked after by Mrs. MacNally while Mom and Annie Rose went to see the doctor. Mrs. MacNally was a very busy person. She did a lot of dusting and polishing and vacuuming, and she cleaned her windows until they sparkled and shone.

That morning Mrs. MacNally was having what she called "a good clear out." So she and Alfie went upstairs, and Alfie pushed his toy cars about on the bedroom floor while Mrs. MacNally pulled everything out of the big cupboard. She folded the shirts and trousers carefully and put them on the bed. Then she started to sort out the rest of the things.

Alfie stopped playing and helped her put the
clothes into different piles. When they found a pair of
Mr. MacNally's socks or gloves, they put them
together. When they found an odd sock or glove,
they put that into another pile until they found the
mate for it. Soon the whole floor, as well as the bed,
was covered with neat piles of matching clothes.

At last, from the very back of the cupboard, Mrs.
MacNally brought out a large black hat.

"Goodness, there's that awful hat!" she said,
dusting it off with her sleeve and holding it up to the
light.

The hat looked quite new. Mrs. MacNally told Alfie that Mr. MacNally had bought it to wear at a very special occasion and that he had paid a lot of money for it. He thought it would "give him height," Mrs. MacNally said. But she didn't think that the hat suited Mr. MacNally well at all. So it had hung, unworn, on the peg in the hall for a long time, until she had taken it down and put it at the very back of the cupboard, where she hoped that Mr. MacNally would forget all about it. And he had.

Alfie thought that Mr. MacNally's hat was a very good hat indeed. He tried it on in front of the big mirror. At first he couldn't see anything at all, but when he pushed it up a bit he could just see out.

While Mrs. MacNally put all the clothes tidily back into the cupboard, Alfie walked up and down in the hat. When Mom came to collect him, Mrs. MacNally said he had been such a good, helpful boy all morning that if he liked he could take the hat home with him and keep it. Alfie thanked Mrs. MacNally and put all his cars into the hat to carry them back across the street.

Alfie liked Mr. MacNally's hat so much that he wore it the rest of the day. It had some dents in it, but he punched them out so that the top was all smooth and rounded. At bedtime he put the hat carefully at the bottom of his bed.

The next morning he wore the hat to nursery school. Mrs. Palmer, his teacher, said that it was such a beautiful hat that it would be safer if Alfie hung it up with the coats while the class was indoors.

But when it was time to go outside in the yard, where the climbing bars and the slide and all the trucks and trolleys were, Alfie put the hat on again. All the other children crowded around and Alfie let them take turns trying it on. Then they invented a very good game in which the person who was wearing the hat ran about, chasing all the other people, and if someone got caught, then it was that person's turn to wear the hat.

For the next few days, Alfie wore the hat a lot.
When he got tired of wearing it, he put it at the
bottom of the toy cupboard where he kept his special
things. Annie Rose found it there and made it into a
bed for her lamb.

But soon they both forgot about the hat altogether.

One of Alfie's very good friends was the milkman. Alfie liked to watch out for him coming down the street in his milk truck. When he came whistling up the steps to leave the milk on the doorstep of Alfie's house, Alfie would wave from the window and the milkman always waved back. And when Mom and Alfie met him out delivering milk around the neighborhood, he would call out: "Watcha mate! How's yourself?"

And Alfie would call back: "Fine thanks, mate!"

Then the milkman would give them a thumbs-up okay sign as he drove on.

In cold weather the milkman sometimes wore a
woolly hat, but the rest of the time he didn't wear
anything on his head. One wet morning, when
the rain was pouring down, Alfie looked out the
window and saw the milkman running up the steps of
their house with all his hair soaking and plastered
down on his forehead. The raindrops were dripping
down his nose and off the end of his beard. Then Alfie
had a very kind thought.

While Mom was paying the milkman, Alfie went to the toy cupboard and brought out Mr. MacNally's black hat. Then he ran to the door.

"Here's a present for you," he said, holding it out. "It's to keep your head dry."

"Thanks a lot," said the milkman, looking at the hat. "That's a good hat, that is," he said. Then he clapped it on his head, went down the steps, and drove off.

But the next time Alfie saw the milkman, he wasn't wearing the hat. Nor the time after that.

"Doesn't he like the hat I gave him?" Alfie asked Mom anxiously.

But Mom said: "Oh, I'm sure he likes it a lot. It's just that the weather's been fine, and I expect he's keeping it for a rainy day."

The next time it rained, Alfie was at the window waiting for the milkman to come down the street. But when at last the milk truck stopped outside Alfie's house and the milkman came up the steps, he still wasn't wearing the hat!

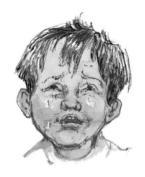

Then Alfie was so upset that he burst into tears. When the milkman saw his sad face at the window, he rang the doorbell, even though it wasn't payday. Mom and Alfie hurried to the door.

"What's up, mate?" the milkman asked Alfie.

"You aren't wearing that hat I gave you," sobbed Alfie.

Then the milkman said: "Come along with me and you'll see why not."

Mom helped Alfie put on his raincoat and his
boots and rainhat, and he and the milkman went out
into the street to where the milk truck was. Then the
milkman hoisted Alfie up and plumped him down
next to the driver's seat.

There on the seat was the hat. Alfie looked inside. And guess what he saw! A little puppy, curled up fast asleep, with his paws over his nose. He had floppy black ears and a black tail.

"He's a stray," the milkman told Alfie. "A lady up the street found him on her doorstep, all wet and shivering. So I took him along with me."

Alfie touched the puppy's back very gently. It felt firm and warm.

"He just got into that hat and settled down as though he'd slept in it all his life," said the milkman. "Me and the wife have been thinking about getting a dog, so if nobody claims him, we'll keep him."

Just then the puppy opened his eyes and licked Alfie's hand. And at that moment Alfie couldn't think of a better use for Mr. MacNally's hat.

Bedtime in Summer

Lying in bed,
not a bit sleepy,
listening to lots of things
going on outside.
People chatting,
and watering their gardens,
and mowing the grass.
Birds calling,
boys shouting,
music from open windows
and a smell of supper.
The sun's still up.
It's slanting in under the curtains.
Alfie wonders —
if he went downstairs —
whether they'd let him stay up, too,
just for a little while.

Here Comes the Bridesmaid

One morning Mom had a letter from her friend Lynn, whom she used to know at work. Lynn wrote that she was going to get married to Harvey Jones and that she wanted them all to come to her wedding. She specially wanted Alfie to be there because she would like him to be her page.

"What's a page?" Alfie wanted to know. "Is it something in a book?"

"No, it's not that kind of page," said Mom, still reading. "It's someone who walks behind the bride in church. There will be two big girls walking with you. They're called bridesmaids."

"But why does Lynn need all those people walking behind her, just because she's marrying Harvey Jones?" asked Alfie.

"Because on that day Lynn will be the bride and a very special person," Mom explained. "She'll wear a long white dress, and you'll have to have a new shirt and a new pair of trousers."

"Is that all I have to do, just walk?" said Alfie. He didn't think that being a page sounded very interesting. But he liked Lynn, and when he heard that after he'd walked behind her in church and been very good and quiet while everyone watched her get married, they would go and have a lovely party with different kinds of cake, he thought that perhaps being a page wouldn't be too bad.

The day before the wedding, Mom took Alfie
down to the church to meet Lynn and the
bridesmaids so that they would all know what to do.
And of course Annie Rose came, too. She and Mom
sat at the back of the church and watched while Lynn
practiced walking up between all the rows of seats to
the front of the church where the minister and
Harvey would be standing, under a window made of
colored glass. Behind her walked Alfie, putting one
foot after the other very slowly and carefully, and
behind him walked the two bridesmaids, side by side.
Alfie had to be specially careful to leave a space
between his feet and Lynn's to make room for the
long dress she was going to wear.

After they'd done this a couple of times, Lynn gave
Alfie a hug and told him he'd got it just right.

That evening Alfie practiced some more. He made
Dad walk up and down wearing a sheet pinned round
his waist and hanging down at the back, in order to
practice not treading on it. Alfie looked hard at
the ground and managed not to step on it, not even
once.

The wedding was at three o'clock the next day. Alfie and Dad, Mom, and Annie Rose arrived early. Alfie, looking extra clean and tidy, stood with the two bridesmaids at the church door, waiting for Lynn. The church was full of people. Harvey was there already, up at the front. Mom, Dad, and Annie Rose sat right at the back.

At last a big shiny car with white ribbons tied on the front drew up. Out got Lynn with her dad. She looked quite different from usual, all dressed up in her long white dress. Alfie thought she was like a princess with a crown of flowers.

Then the music played very loudly and everyone stood up. Lynn took her dad's arm and they all began to walk very slowly up the aisle to where Harvey was waiting. It was just as they had practiced it, except that now all the people were looking at them. But Alfie kept his eyes straight ahead. He was being careful not to tread on Lynn's beautiful white dress.

Halfway up the aisle, Alfie felt something behind him, tugging at the back of his shirt.

Then Alfie felt a little hand in his. It was Annie Rose! She had joined the wedding procession and was toddling happily up the aisle beside Alfie.

Alfie glanced round. He saw Mom looking at him, and he looked back at her. They both knew Annie Rose rather well. They knew that if Mom came and picked her up to take her back to her seat, she would scream. She might even lie down in the middle of the church and go all stiff and drum her feet on the floor! Alfie knew how terrible that would be.

So he turned round again and walked on, holding Annie Rose's hand tightly, and she walked beside him, as good as gold. She had watched him practicing and knew just what to do.

When they reached Harvey and the minister, the music stopped and they all stood still. But Mom had slipped up to the front of the church, and when Annie Rose saw her nearby, she calmly let go of Alfie's hand and trotted over to her.

Annie Rose was very good and quiet all through the talking and singing and prayers. But when at last the wedding service was over and Lynn and Harvey walked, smiling, arm in arm, out of the church, Annie Rose struggled out of Mom's arms and joined in behind them, next to Alfie. And she was just as careful as he was not to tread on Lynn's dress.

Outside in the sunshine the church bells rang out. Lynn and Harvey stood on the steps while a man took photographs. The bridesmaids stood on either side and Lynn and Harvey in the middle. Then Lynn made Annie Rose stand next to Alfie, right in front, for a picture.

Afterward they all went to a big room where a lot of beautiful food was laid out. There was a white wedding cake with a silver horseshoe on top. Alfie had two kinds of cake and some strawberries. Annie Rose had a chocolate cream roll.

"I didn't know I was going to have three bridesmaids," said Lynn, laughing. "But I guess three is a much luckier number than two!"

Birthday

Tomorrow there's going to be:
Hugs and kisses,
cards in the mail,
probably balloons,
a big cake with icing
and candles,
chocolate cookies,
potato chips,
ice cream,
and lots of presents.
Alfie's friends are all coming tomorrow,
and they'll all have to be
specially nice to him
because it's going to be
Alfie's Birthday!